Encouraging CONFIDENCE

Learning to not be SHY

Jasmine Brooke

FOX EYE
PUBLISHING

Rhino found it difficult to be **CONFIDENT**. He could be a little **SHY**.

Rhino found it hard to **SPEAK UP**.

He found it difficult to meet someone new.

But being **SHY** meant Rhino missed out. It made him feel **SCARED**, too.

On Tuesday, Mrs Tree suggested that everyone could write a poem. Then she added, "Perhaps we could read them **OUT LOUD?**"

"Oooh, yes!" screeched Monkey. She loved to **SHOW OFF** her work. Lion smiled, thinking, "I'll be the star of the show!"

Rhino picked up his pen, **WORRYING** the whole time. He was too **SHY** to **SHOW OFF** like Monkey. Too **SCARED** to be the star of the show.

Monkey read her poem with **CONFIDENCE**. Parrot spoke so well, and when Lion took his turn, he really did steal the show.

Rhino **QUIVERED** in his seat. He knew his turn had come. He held up his poem. He opened his mouth to speak. But Rhino was so **SHY**, not a single word came out!

"I'm too **SHY**," Rhino sighed, "to be the star of any show."

When school was over, Mrs Tree read Rhino's poem. It was written with such **CONFIDENCE**. It had been written so well.

"Of all the poems in the class," thought Mrs Tree, "Rhino's stole the show."

The next morning, Mrs Tree said, "Let's try something new." She drew the stage curtains, then smiled at Rhino, "Why not give it a go?"

Behind the curtains, Rhino didn't feel **SHY**. Not one bit. He read his poem with **CONFIDENCE**. He spoke so very well.

The class clapped and clapped. They cheered on Rhino. Then, feeling **BRAVER**, Rhino pulled back the curtains ...

Rhino could clearly see he was the star of the show!

Mrs Tree smiled as Rhino read with **CONFIDENCE** and tried something new. She laughed when Rhino took a bow and waved to the crowd. At last, Rhino had learnt to show just what he could do.

The next day, Mrs Tree suggested that the class try something new. "I think we should put on a play," she smiled to Rhino. "What about you?"

Monkey played her part, and Lion took on his role. But now that he was not so **SHY**, it was Rhino who stole the show!

Words and feelings

Rhino felt very shy in this story. That made him feel scared and that held Rhino back.

There are a lot of words to do with feeling shy and learning to be confident in this book. Can you remember all of them?

BRAVER

SPEAK UP

Let's talk about behaviour

This series helps children to understand and manage difficult emotions and behaviours. The animal characters in the series have been created to show human behaviour that is often seen in young children, and which they may find difficult to manage.

Encouraging Confidence

The story in this book examines issues around feeling shy and lacking confidence. It looks at how not being confident can mean that people do not try new things and then lose out.

The book is designed to show young children how they can manage their behaviour and learn to be confident.

How to use this book

You can read this book with one child or a group of children. The book can be used to begin a discussion around complex behaviour such as developing confidence.

The book is also a reading aid, with enlarged and repeated words to help children to develop their reading skills.

How to read the story

Before beginning the story, ensure that the children you are reading to are relaxed and focused.

Take time to look at the enlarged words and the illustrations, and discuss what this book might be about before reading the story.

New words can be tricky for young children to approach. Sounding them out first, slowly and repeatedly, can help children to learn the words and become familiar with them.

How to discuss the story

When you have finished reading the story, use these questions and discussion points to examine the theme of the story with children and explore the emotions and behaviours within it:

- What do you think the story was about? Have you been in a situation in which you were shy and found it hard to be confident? What was that situation? For example, did you not take part in a play or another performance? Encourage the children to talk about their experiences.
- Talk about ways that people can overcome feeling shy. For example, by trying small actions first such as speaking up in front of family and friends before learning to talk to new people. Talk to the children about what tools they think might work for them and why.
- Discuss the problems that result from feeling shy and not being confident. Explain that Rhino was shy and lacking in confidence in the story, and that made him nervous and anxious.
- Talk about why it is important to learn to be confident. Discuss the value of doing so.

Titles in the series

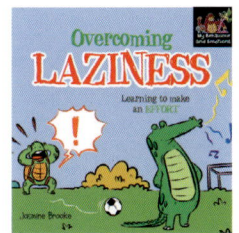 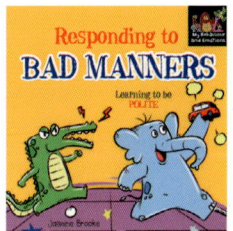 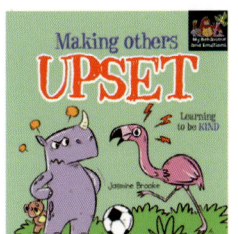 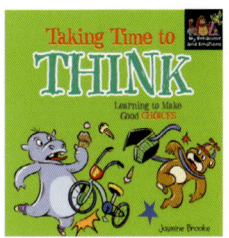 

 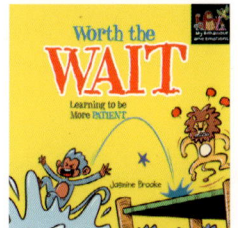 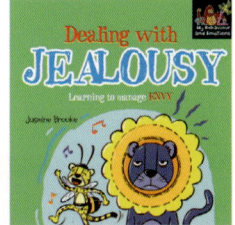  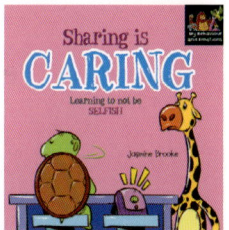

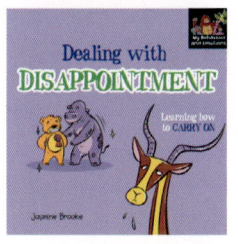 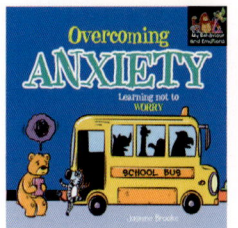 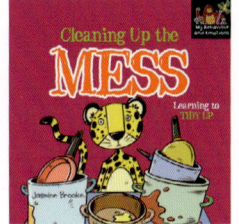  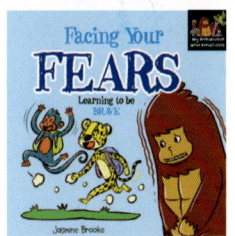

  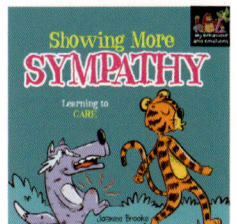 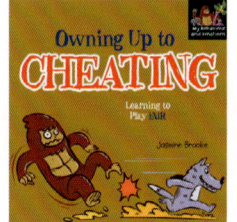 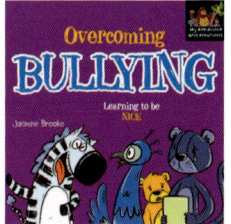

First published in 2023 by Fox Eye Publishing
Unit 31, Vulcan House Business Centre,
Vulcan Road, Leicester, LE5 3EF
www.foxeyepublishing.com

Copyright © 2023 Fox Eye Publishing
All rights reserved. No portion of this book may be reproduced in any form without permission from the publisher, except as permitted by U.K. copyright law.

Author: Jasmine Brooke
Art director: Paul Phillips
Cover designer: Emma Bailey & Salma Thadha
Editor: Jenny Rush

All illustrations by Novel

ISBN 978-1-80445-289-9

A catalogue record for this book is available from the British Library

Printed in China